MUM'S W

Mum is mad about enter what the prize. Wh
wins anything anyway.   Angie's four-
leaved clover suddenly works its magic and Angie
and her dad find themselves sharing their home
with Mum's extraordinary prizes. A year's supply
of baby rusks and cat food would be quite useful —
if they had either a baby or a cat — but the house
really isn't big enough for so many tins.

Nor is it big enough for Wallace Windle, an ageing,
self-important film star. He used to be Mum's
favourite . . . but she lives to regret ever winning
the chance to have dinner with him.

This is a very funny book indeed about the dangers
of entering one competition too many.

David Wiseman was born in Manchester and grew
up there. After serving in the forces, he became a
teacher and then a headmaster in Cornwall, where
he lives still.

DAVID WISEMAN

Mum's Winning Streak

Illustrated by Terry McKenna

PUFFIN BOOKS
in association with Blackie

For Lael
and
Sooch, Figaro, Sheba,
Polly, Suki, Snuff, Pompom,
Soochka and Soochong,
Scott, Sasha, Shoshone and Su-li.

PUFFIN BOOKS

Published by the Penguin Group
Penguin Books Ltd, 27 Wrights Lane, London W8 5TZ, England
Penguin Books USA Inc., 375 Hudson Street, New York, New York 10014, USA
Penguin Books Australia Ltd, Ringwood, Victoria, Australia
Penguin Books Canada Ltd, 10 Alcorn Avenue, Toronto, Ontario, Canada M4V 3B2
Penguin Books (NZ) Ltd, 182–190 Wairau Road, Auckland 10, New Zealand

Penguin Books Ltd, Registered Offices: Harmondsworth, Middlesex, England

First published in Blackie Snappers by Blackie and Son Limited 1990
Published in Puffin Books 1992
1 3 5 7 9 10 8 6 4 2

Text copyright © David Wiseman, 1990
Illustrations copyright © Terry McKenna, 1990
All rights reserved

The moral right of the author has been asserted

Printed in England by Clays Ltd, St Ives plc

1 . . .

It all started on holiday when Angie found a four-leaved clover.

It had rained most of the time and their caravan was miles from the discos and cafés. Angie had done nothing but stare moodily out to sea, go for walks in the rain, or, when the rain eased, go with Dad for a round on the miniature golf course. And Dad always won.

Until she found the four-leaved clover.

'That's lucky, that is,' said Mum. 'And it's already brought fine weather.' The rain had stopped and a weak sun showed through a mist of cloud.

'Come on, Angie. Golf,' said Dad with a burst of enthusiasm.

Angie was tired of being beaten. What fun was there in a game which she always lost?

'Get a move on,' Dad called. 'Let's make the most of the weather.' She followed him to the miniature golf course where other gloomy holiday-makers, wrapped in anoraks against the wind, were already playing.

Dad teed off first and hit his ball into a bunker. That usually happened to Angie. This time she swung her club and the ball sailed on to the green and to Angie's amazement – and Dad's annoyance – disappeared down the hole.

'Ah well, if you're going to play like that,' said Dad, pretending he'd landed in the bunker on purpose, to give Angie a chance, 'I'll have to take things seriously.' It took him three shots to sink his ball.

Angie took the first stroke next. Her ball left the tee like a bullet, struck a tree, rebounded on to the green, trickled towards the second hole, hesitated, and toppled in.

'I don't believe it,' said Dad, and his temper wasn't improved when he took five shots for a hole that usually took him two.

At the next hole there was a stream a few yards from the tee. Angie's ball had always landed in it before, but this time she drove over it and her ball sailed towards hole number three out of sight round a bend in the course. Dad mis-hit; his ball bounced once, twice and went, splash, into the stream. It took him three more shots to get near the hole.

'Ah!' he said when he saw no sign of Angie's ball. 'You've gone into the gorse bushes, I expect. You'll never get out.' He rubbed his hands in triumph.

'Here it is,' said Angie, picking her ball out of the hole. 'Another hole in one.'

She was enjoying the game and the more she enjoyed it, the more surely her ball flew to its target, and the more angry Dad became; his swings became wilder and by the eighth hole he was so mad he tried to break his club across his knee, but all he did was injure himself. His face twisted with frustration as Angie holed in one again.

'It's a childish game,' he said. 'I've had enough.' He stormed off and Angie went on to the last and ninth hole, sank her ball in one, followed her father to hand in club and ball at the grounds-man's hut and went back to the caravan.

'Well?' said Mum. 'How many did you win by today, dear?'

Dad scowled. 'It was Angie's turn today,' he said as if he had lost deliberately.

'Oh, that's nice, Angie,' said Mum.

'Just luck, Mum,' said Angie.

'Well of course, dear. You had your four-leaved clover.'

'That's it,' said Dad, recovering his good humour. 'Luck, that's all it was. The four-leaved clover.'

Angie returned home from her holiday with the clover in an envelope to keep it safe.

Angie didn't think a mere plant could bring luck but she didn't throw it away. Then at a fête she won a box of chocolates in a raffle and correctly guessed the number of peas in a jar.

'I don't believe it,' she told herself, but that night she slept with the clover under her pillow. When she woke up a sort of slogan was running through her mind: 'Riley's Rusks are Right Good Grub'. She couldn't get it out of her head. It was still there at breakfast, so when her mother said, 'Good morning, Angie,' she answered, 'Riley's Rusks are Right Good Grub.'

'What nonsense!' said Dad. 'You must be off your rocker.' He was never at his best in the morning.

'Be quiet, dear,' Mum said. 'What was that, Angie?'

Angie repeated her bit of nonsense. 'Riley's Rusks are Right Good Grub.'

'That couldn't be better,' said Mum. She searched among a pile of magazines, found *Woman's Sphere*, and opened it at an advertisement for Riley's Rusks.

'Not another competition,' groaned Dad. 'When will you learn? You never win.'

Angie agreed. Mum entered every possible competition: a holiday abroad, groceries for life, signed photographs of pop stars, it did not matter to her what the prizes were, it was the entering that thrilled her. She wasn't disappointed that she never won. There was always another competition to enter. She bought any product running a competition until the kitchen cupboards were filled with tins and jars of every kind, their contents a mystery, since all the labels had been removed to go with the competition entries.

'Say it again, dear,' Mum said.

'Riley's Rusks are Right Good Grub.'

'There you are,' said Mum. 'Look at that lovely baby. Isn't that just what he's saying?' A photograph showed a baby clutching a biscuit and, beside it, the words 'Tell us what he's saying and win a year's supply of Riley's Rusks for *your* baby'.

'But we haven't got a baby,' said Angie.

Mum looked at her in surprise. 'What's that got to do with it?'

'What would we do with a year's supply of rusks?' said Angie.

'It won't win anyway,' said Dad.

It did win. Several weeks later a large van stopped

at their gate and a dapper man in a neat blue suit leapt out and knocked at the door.

'Mrs Potter?' he said as Angie opened the door.

'That's me,' said Mum over Angie's shoulder.

'Riley's Rusks are Right Good Grub,' he said and beamed. 'My name's Hoggins, madam. I'm happy to tell you you've won the Riley Baby contest.' He gestured at the van. 'There's your year's supply. I'll tell the driver to bring it in. There's just one thing left.' He had a camera at the ready. 'Just the photograph.'

Mum smirked and patted her hair. 'Oh, I must tidy up. I'm not fit to have my photo—'

'Oh not you, madam, the baby.'

'The baby?'

'You did read the rules? The winner agrees to allow photographs of her baby to be used to advertise Riley's Rusks.'

'Oh, the baby. Just a minute.' Mum closed the door on the man and whispered to Angie 'Go to Mrs Roberts and borrow Tommy. Quickly now.'

'Tommy?'

'Don't be awkward, Angie. We need a baby. Get me one quickly. Tommy if you can, but anyone'll do.'

'Oh, Mum!' Angie protested but ran out of the

back of the house to Mrs Roberts next door. Mrs Roberts had seven children, including two sets of twins. Tommy, the youngest, was a large round-faced eight-month old with a voracious appetite. He was on the floor of the living-room surrounded by his brothers and sisters, all talking at once.

'Can I borrow Tommy?' Angie shouted.

Mrs Roberts lifted her head from her ironing. 'Take the lot,' she said. 'Keep 'em as long as you like – a couple of years if you want.'

'Just Tommy for half an hour.' She picked him up and ran back home. Tommy chortled.

'Here you are, Mum.' She handed Tommy over. He liked Angie's mum; she was warm and cosy and always had time to spare for him.

'Here you are,' Mum said, opening the door to Mr Hoggins.

'He's a big chap,' said the man.

Tommy behaved perfectly, chewing one rusk after another.

'What's his name?' said Mr Hoggins when he had taken the last photograph.

'Tommy Roberts,' Mum said without thinking, then quickly added 'Tommy Robert Potter.'

'Right, Tommy Robert Potter,' said Hoggins, picking Tommy up and throwing him in the air

and catching him. 'You'll be famous.' Tommy, overfull with Riley's Rusks, burped, gulped and brought up most of the rusks over the nice man's smart blue suit.

Mr Hoggins left hurriedly, avoiding Tommy's grasping hands. The van driver brought in crates and cartons, filling the hall, the stairs and third bedroom with Riley's Rusks.

Angie's mum looked at the stacks with pride. 'There,' she said. 'I knew I'd win one day.'

Angie shook her head. 'What use are all these rusks to us?'

'Mrs Potter will be glad of them. They'll be Tommy's reward for being such a good boy,' Mum said. 'Right Good Grub, eh, Tommy?' Tommy reached for another rusk. He meant to make the most of his good luck.

2 . . .

'We're on a winning streak,' Mum said and bought every magazine with a competition in it. She sat studying them while Angie got on with her homework.

'Here's one worth winning,' Mum said. Angie tried to ignore her but it was no use. She picked up her books to take them to her bedroom and do her work there.

'No, Angie, listen. You're good at these things. Remember Riley's Rusks.'

She couldn't forget them. They were everywhere.

'You can do this, I'm sure. Write a limerick about a cat food called Mews.'

'What's the prize?' growled Dad. 'A year's supply of cat food I suppose, when we haven't even got a cat.'

Mum shook her head at his lack of enterprise. 'It doesn't matter what the prize is. It's going in for it that's the thing. It keeps the brain active. Start thinking, Angie.'

That's right, thought Angie, it's my brain that's to be activated.

'A limerick, Angie. You could do that easily.'

'I'll try,' she said. 'When I've finished my maths.' She went upstairs to do her homework but began to think of limericks instead. The first line was to be 'There's nothing so tasty as Mews'. But she couldn't get any further. She wrote all the words she could think of to rhyme with Mews – cruise, crews, twos, zoos, bruise. Inspiration wouldn't come and she decided maths was easier. She finished her homework and went downstairs.

'Got it, Angie, love?' her mother asked.

She shook her head.

'I have,' said Dad. 'Listen to this:

There's nothing so tasty as Mews
To go with a good drop of booze;
    A bottle of brown
    Will help it go down—

'Until all your senses you lose,' interrupted Mum angrily. 'You can't take anything seriously, can you?'

Dad looked shamefaced. 'Well—' he began.

'Well, nothing.' Mum was angry, not at Dad, Angie thought, but at their failure to think of a winning limerick.

16

The next morning, Saturday, Angie went shopping with Mum. At the supermarket Mum searched the shelves for any goods advertising competitions.

She's gone mad, Angie thought, as her mother gathered all manner of things they would never use. 'There,' Mum said, putting three cans into the trolley. 'Three labels is all you need to enter.'

'What are they, Mum?'

Mum looked surprised. '*I* don't know. Oh yes, snails it says.'

'Ugh!' said Angie. 'We don't eat snails.'

'We don't need to eat them. It's the labels.'

'Oh, Mum,' said Angie. 'I give up.'

But Mum didn't give up. She bought four tins of Mews cat food, three kinds of soup, a new brand of dog food – and a large packet of dishwasher powder. And we haven't a dishwasher, Angie was about to say, but knew it would be pointless arguing.

They turned to collect their regular provisions. 'I don't know where the money goes,' Mum said when she saw the size of the bill.

When they reached home Mum removed all the labels needed for competition entries. Then she put the tins, now unrecognisable as cat or dog food, or fruit, or soup, into the cupboards to join the other anonymous tins already stocked there.

Angie sighed. 'Mum, you'll never know what you've got.'

'It makes it so much more interesting. You think you're opening a tin of tomato soup and it turns out to be peaches.'

'Or snails,' said Angie.

'Or snails,' said her mother, gathering all the labels together. 'Let me see, a trip on Concorde, a new car, a dream house. What will it be?' Her eyes were bright with the thought of winning. She settled on the labels for Mews, the cat food.

'Get your thinking cap on, Angie,' she urged.

'We don't want lots of cat food,' Angie said. 'We haven't a cat and neither has Mrs Roberts, so you can't use her again.'

'You never know,' said Mum. 'It may come in useful one day. Where shall we put it?' She spoke as if the competition was already won.

At lunch Mum said, 'I wanted to give you mushy peas, but I opened four tins and two turned out to be mulligatawny soup and two were pears. So it's pears for pudding and soup for supper. It all works out in the end. And you must think of something soon, Angie. The closing date is a week today.'

It was all very well for Mum to say competitions kept the brain working. When it came to anything difficult she always turned to Angie.

Angie didn't like to disappoint her mother so she went to her bedroom to think of the limerick, but nothing would come. She started to tidy her

19

room instead and came across the envelope with the four-leaved clover. She'd forgotten about it. Perhaps that would bring her ideas for a rhyme, she thought, but it didn't work. She put the whole thing out of her head.

That evening there was no mention of cat food or competitions. Dad held forth about a film they'd seen on television.

'Where did they unearth that old rubbish?' he complained.

'Oh, it was lovely,' said Mum. 'And wasn't Wallace Windle wonderful?' She sighed. 'If only I could meet him. Such a handsome man.'

Dad snorted. 'If you like that sort of thing.'

Angie smiled. Dad pretended to be an old curmudgeon but he put up with Mum's competitions without too much grumbling and if mushy peas turned up instead of pears, or pears instead of mushy peas, he didn't complain. He might not be so good-tempered if snails appeared instead of beef stew or dog food instead of baked beans, though.

She went to bed and woke in the morning saying to herself:

'There's nothing so tasty as Mews.

It beats all your roast beef or stews.

> There isn't a cat
> That doesn't think that
> It deserves to come first on the news.'

She didn't know where the limerick had come from, but there it was. It might not be a winner but it would please Mum.

'Of course it's a winner,' said Mum. 'Just as it is.' She collected up the labels, filled out the entry form and went to the post with it.

The cat food arrived on a Friday afternoon and they spent most of the weekend finding room for their winnings. By the time they had finished, cartons were everywhere, under the kitchen table, on top of the TV, stacked ceiling high in the lavatory. Dad went there and, shortly after, a cry of agony burst from within. Mum and Angie rushed upstairs and Mum pushed the door open. Dad was on the loo, trousers down below his knees, with tins of cat food cascading about him.

'Ow!' he yelled as a tin cracked him on the head. 'And don't stand there laughing. Shut the door. Let me examine my injuries in dignity.'

He came downstairs rubbing his head and, to their surprise, smiling as he recited:

> 'I feel I must tell you the loo's

No place for the storage of Mews.

    I've come out in lumps

    And blisters and bumps,

   And just take a look at this bruise.'

He bent his head for Mum to examine the damage. He moaned in agony.

'We'll have to do something about all those tins,' he said through cries of distress as Mum dabbed his cuts with iodine.

'Of course, dear,' said Mum. 'We'll get a cat.'

'We'll need an army of cats to get rid of that lot,' Dad said.

'Or one very greedy cat,' said Angie.

'Competitions!' Dad said when Mum had finished repairing him. 'That's the lot.'

'If you say so, dear,' said Mum, with suspiciously quick agreement.

Later she gave Angie an envelope. 'Slip to the post with it, Angie. It was already filled in. I couldn't waste it, could I?'

'What's it for, Mum?' Angie said. 'Not a year's supply of anything, I hope.'

'Just you wait and see,' said Mum.

3 . . .

Though Angie thought Mum's competitions were harmless, it was a nuisance having cartons and boxes on the stairs, piled against the walls, cluttering every room. There was hardly space left for themselves.

'We'd better get a cat,' Angie said.

'Where would we put him?' Dad asked, stretching out his legs and knocking over a stack of tins.

'We'll make room,' said Mum. 'Go to the Animal Shelter, Angie. They'll have a stray. Choose a nice one, dear.'

'Get a big one,' Dad said. 'One that'll eat its way quickly through this lot.'

So Angie went to the cat shelter. A big one, Dad had said. A big one it must be.

'What sort do you want?' the girl attendant asked. 'We've black ones, white ones, fluffy ones, smooth ones. Take your pick.'

'Just a big and greedy one,' said Angie.

'We've got the very one,' the girl said, trying to hide her delight. She led Angie to a cage away from the rest. 'There,' she said. 'He's what you need.'

Angie looked at the cat and the cat looked at Angie. His eyes were green and baleful. He was black and sleek and stretched up to the front of the cage when Angie drew near. He was big, with long legs, powerful shoulders and he opened his mouth in an enormous yawn, showing white gleaming fangs.

'Is he all right?' Angie said.

'What do you mean, all right?'

'He looks fierce.'

The girl opened the cage and the cat stalked

out, tail erect, eyed Angie, rubbed against her legs
and purred.

'What's his name?' Angie said.

'We call him Goliath.'

'Does he eat a lot?'

'He's never satisfied, but—' The girl looked
anxiously at Angie. 'I'm sure that's because he's
got nothing else to do here but eat.'

'You don't understand,' said Angie. 'We want
a big eater.'

The girl smiled. 'You've got him.'

Angie borrowed a basket and walked to the bus
stop with Goliath. Throughout the ride, blood-
curdling growls came from the basket. The
woman sitting next to Angie looked uneasy.

'What's in there?' she asked. 'A tiger cub?'

'Only a cat,' Angie replied.

'I don't believe it,' said the woman.

Goliath snarled and the woman blenched and
moved away.

'Is he safe in there?' she asked.

'I hope so,' Angie said. The woman grew even
paler and rose to leave the bus. 'It'll do me good
to walk,' she said and scuttled away as Goliath's
growls rose to match the sound of the bus's engine.

'Ssh—' Angie said. 'Behave yourself!' But Goli-

ath went on growling until they arrived at her stop.

'I've got him,' she announced at home.

'I hope he's a big one,' Dad said.

Angie opened the basket and, with one athletic movement, Goliath leapt out and stood glaring around him. His eyes met Dad's.

'Oh no,' said Dad. He moved back a pace and fell sprawling over a carton. Goliath advanced.

'Keep him off! Keep him off' Dad cried.

'What's all the fuss?' Mum said, coming from the kitchen. She saw Goliath and exclaimed, 'Oh, isn't he beautiful?' She knelt down and stroked him. He wound his graceful body about her legs, purring as loudly now as he had growled before.

Dad rose to his feet and stood as far from Goliath as he could. 'Well, he's big, I'll say that.'

'I'll give him some Mews,' Angie said. Goliath followed her and when she put the dish of Mews before him he sniffed at it, looked crossly up at Angie and walked disdainfully away.

'I was saving some pork for our tea,' Mum said. 'See if he'd like that, Angie.'

'Not likely,' Dad said, but, when Goliath turned and glared, he said, 'All right. Give him our tea, Angie. But keep him away from me.'

'He won't eat you,' Mum said.

'How do you know?' Dad said. He watched Goliath finish the pork joint until, satisfied, the cat strode into the living room, surveyed his new home, made his way to Dad's chair, jumped on it, turned around a few times, washed himself, curled up, and went to sleep.

'That's my chair,' Dad said.

'I don't suppose he'd mind sharing it with you,' Mum said.

Dad looked crossly at her and then at Goliath. He went to his chair to move the cat aside. Goliath opened an eye, twitched his tail, said something

under his breath, and Dad retreated.

Goliath would have nothing to do with Mews. He insisted on sharing their pork, or beef, or chicken. Dad was indignant.

'See where your competitions have landed us,' he grumbled. 'Eaten out of house and home by a cat. And look at him.'

Goliath stretched lazily on Dad's chair.

'Why did we get him?' Dad said. 'To get rid of

all this cat food. And what have we got instead?

Goliath won't look at his Mews,
The smell of it gives him the blues,
But he loves our roast lamb,
Our prime beef or ham,
And then collars my chair for a snooze.

'My chair,' he repeated. '*My* chair. Take him back, Angie. If he won't eat Mews, he's no good to us.'

'Don't be silly, dear,' Mum said. 'We can get rid of the cat food, but not the cat. Goliath has come to stay, haven't you?' Goliath raised his head to be stroked.

Dad looked pleadingly at Angie. 'You don't want him, do you, Angie?'

Angie looked at Dad, then at Goliath. 'I'm afraid so, Dad.'

'I give up,' said Dad.

'I knew you'd be sensible,' said Mum.

'I think the Animal Welfare people would be glad of the food,' Angie said.

'Why didn't you think of that before we got *him*?' Dad said, glaring at Goliath.

Goliath purred with contentment and went to sleep.

* * *

The cat shelter people were delighted to take the cat food and the house began to return to normal – apart from Goliath's presence. He dominated the household; his needs shaped their lives.

'We'll get chicken this weekend,' Mum said when she went shopping on Saturday. 'Goliath could do with a change.'

Angie knew Mum was still sending in entries for all sorts of competitions. New tins, without labels, appeared in the pantry, and surprises met them at every meal. Dad still didn't complain. He even pretended to like sitting on a hard-backed chair instead of his old familiar easy chair. But once or twice Angie caught him eyeing Goliath with murderous intent. She was glad Dad wasn't a violent man. In any case, in a fight between Dad and Goliath, it wouldn't be Dad who won.

Goliath terrorised the neighbourhood. No other cats – or dogs – had been near the house since he came. And the milkman begged Mum to 'keep that creature away'.

Tommy Roberts loved him and showed it by pulling his tail, tweaking his ears, prodding and pushing him. Goliath purred and came back for more. Dad suggested they should give Goliath to Tommy. 'For good,' he said. 'My good.'

'No,' said Mum. 'He's ours and he stays. See if he likes sausages, Angie. I think we can spare him some from our tea.'

He liked sausages. He liked anything they ate, thought he had a right to share in whatever the family had.

He only had one difference of opinion with Mum.

She insisted on watching every old film of Wallace Windle's.

'Not again, Mum,' Angie pleaded.

'Oh, not again,' Dad implored.

Mum ignored them and switched on the TV. Wallace Windle emerged on the screen – dark shining hair, sleek black moustache, flashing smile.

'Isn't he gorgeous?' Mum said, drooling.

Goliath got up from his chair, approached the television, spat in anger, then – when Wallace Windle did not disappear – he jumped on the top of the set and, with outstretched paw, tried to scoop the actor from the screen.

'Goliath!' Mum called. 'Behave yourself!' But she had to pick him up and put him out of the room. They heard him growling in fury as he leapt at the door handle.

'See what he wants, Angie,' Mum said.

'He wants you to switch off, Mum. He doesn't like Wallace Windle.'

'Nonsense. Nobody could dislike him.'

'I do,' said Dad.

Angie took Goliath to her bedroom but, whenever the sound of Windle's voice reached them, he snarled menacingly.

'It's all right, Goliath,' Angie reassured him. 'Wallace Windle's only a picture. He's not real.'

Goliath was not appeased but, when music heralded the end of the film, he became calm enough to be allowed back into the living-room.

Dad was sitting in his old chair. Goliath eyed him. Dad hurriedly returned to the hard-backed chair on the other side of the fireplace. Goliath leapt to the easy chair, stretched and yawned.

'What's happened to this house?' Dad muttered. 'Eh?'

Goliath purred.

4 . . .

'Have you seen my four-leaved clover, Mum?'
Angie asked.

'I meant to tell you dear. I borrowed it. For
something personal.'

'What sort of thing?

Mum smiled, and there was a light in her eyes
as if something exciting was about to happen. It
couldn't just be the approach of Christmas.

'What is it, Mum?' Angie asked.

'You just wait,' Mum said, giving a little shiver
of delight. 'It worked,' she said, handing the four-
leaved clover back to Angie. 'It worked for me
too.'

Dad was still wary of Goliath. Angie could not
understand why. Goliath was such a gentle creature really. He let Tommy Roberts do whatever
he wanted, purring ecstatically as Tommy pulled
him about.

Tommy was a frequent visitor. Mum was happy
to have him and Mrs Roberts was glad to get him

off her hands for an hour or two. Tommy was so good-natured he loved everyone. He even liked Wallace Windle. Once when a Wallace Windle film came on in the afternoon Tommy watched it throughout, gurgling with joy whenever the actor appeared.

'You see,' said Mum. 'Some people appreciate charm and elegance. You do, don't you, Tommy?'

Tommy burped loudly.

'Out of the mouths of babes and sucklings,' said Dad.

Mum looked daggers at him. 'You can't stop me,' she said cryptically.

'She's up to something,' Dad said to Angie. 'And I don't like it. You've not been helping her with one of her competitions, Angie?'

'No,' said Angie. But Mum had borrowed the four-leaved clover for 'something personal'. Perhaps she'd entered one on her own. Perhaps she'd even won.

Mum's habits changed. She became fussy about the house, getting rid of newspapers before they'd even been read, brushing down the stairs twice a day, cleaning the windows every other day, polishing furniture, dusting everywhere.

'Woman!' protested Dad, but without effect. She went on, making everyone move – even Goliath – so that she could straighten the cushions.

She went to town and bought herself a smart off-the-shoulder dress of blue and gold. She brought a wallpaper-pattern book home, chose a bright floral paper and insisted on Dad spending the weekend decorating the living-room.

'What's it all about, Mum?' Angie demanded.

Mum giggled and blushed like a schoolgirl asked about her first love affair.

'Oh, Mum!' Angie said, exasperated.

On Monday Mum came back from town with her hair set in a perm and Angie knew something unusual was in the wind.

'You look very nice, love,' Dad said. 'Is the Queen coming to visit?'

'Can't I make something of myself if I want to?' Mum said crossly.

'You look lovely, Mum,' Angie told her, but she also wondered if someone was expected. Mum had never had her hair permed before. It was not the sort of hair that needed it.

The following afternoon and evening Mum got more and more restless.

'Leave it,' Dad said, when for the tenth time Mum dusted the television set and plumped the chair cushions. 'What's got into you?'

'You'll see,' Mum said. She had changed into her new dress and stood before the mirror patting her hair and preening herself.

There was a knock at the front door. 'I'll go,' Angie said and, before her mother could move, went to the door.

A man stood there. There was something familiar about him, though Angie could not think where she had seen him before. He was small and round, pear-shaped, little legs under a fat bottom. He had side-whiskers of an unnatural black, heavy jowls, a pale face, thick red lips.

'My dear,' he said in a sonorous voice, taking off his broad-brimmed black hat with a dramatic sweep. 'How darlingly sweet of you to remember an old Thespian like me. I am deeply flattered.'

Something about the voice brought Wallace Windle to mind. But Wallace Windle on film was tall and slender, dashing and debonair, young and handsome.

This Wallace Windle was fat and oily, small and smug, his smooth dark hair an obvious toupee.

'Oh, Mr Windle,' Angie heard Mum sigh behind her. 'Oh, Mr Windle, do come in. What an honour to meet you.'

'The honour is all mine, dear lady.' He looked at Angie. 'And this lovely girl must be your sister, if you are Rosemary Potter.'

'Oh yes. I'm Rosemary Potter,' Mum simpered. 'But this is my daughter Angie.'

'Your daughter? I cannot believe it, Rosemary. I may call you Rosemary?' He gestured with every word.

'Who is it?' Dad called. 'Shut the door. There's a hell of a draught.'

Mum reddened with embarrassment, but Wallace Windle was not put out. He advanced without hesitation into the living-room, and halted.

Angie thought it was the sight of Dad that brought him to a stop, but it was Goliath arching his back and spitting with venom as he recognised the actor.

'Take him out, Angie,' Mum said in horror and, as Angie carried Goliath away, Mum turned in apology. 'He's not our cat really,' she said. 'Just a stray we took in.'

Dad looked accusingly at her.

'I've taken him to play with Tommy,' Angie said on her return.

The actor was looking round the room with raised eyebrows. 'A delightful room,' he said. 'So old-world.' Dad scowled. 'And now, dear lady, the carriage awaits.'

'The carriage?' said Dad.

'The Rolls, darling,' Windle said to Dad.

'Please, Dad,' Angie whispered, thinking Dad was about to explode.

'I should have explained,' Mum said. 'Mr Windle—

'Wallace,' he interrupted. 'Call me Wallace, my dear Rosemary.'

Dad scowled again but the actor didn't notice.

'Yes, er, Wallace,' Mum said. 'Wallace is taking me out to dinner. I won an evening out with my favourite film star.'

'And I have come to claim it,' said Windle in a

dramatic voice. 'The privilege is all mine. Shall we?' He gestured flamboyantly towards the door, took Mum's arm and led her away.

'I'll be—,' Dad said.

5 . . .

Angie did not hear her mother come back. Nor did she see her in the morning before going to school. She could not get a word out of Dad at breakfast. He was never good in the mornings, but he was even less talkative than usual.

In the afternoon Angie came home to find her mother singing her way about the house, songs from Wallace Windle films about moonlight and love and romance.

'What are we having for tea, Mum?' Angie asked.

'Tea?' Mum said dreamily. 'Oh, open a tin of something. I couldn't eat a thing.'

'What did you have last night?' Angie was curious to know what had happened.

'Oh! Last night!' Mum sighed.

'What did you have to eat? Where did you go?'

'Eat? I didn't notice.'

'Didn't you eat anything?' Angie said.

'Of course we ate. Don't talk nonsense. I just can't think what we had. It was so wonderful.'

'What was he like?'

Mum opened her eyes wide. 'Like? What do you expect? All that a man should be.'

Angie wondered if she and Mum had seen the same Wallace Windle.

'We must do up the spare room,' Mum said. 'It's not been painted for years.'

Angie looked at Mum with suspicion. Why should the spare room need decorating?

'Your father can do it this weekend,' Mum said. 'He likes that sort of work.'

'Well?' Dad said when he got home. 'Have you got any sense out of her, Angie?'

'Are you talking about me?' Mum said.

'Ah!' said Dad. 'You are back in the real world, then?'

Mum smiled as if she had memories she could not possibly share with him.

'She wants you to do up the spare room,' Angie said. Mum glared crossly at her.

'I was going to choose my moment.' Mum looked pleadingly at Dad. 'It does need it, you know.'

'Why now?' Dad said. 'Just before Christmas, when there's so much else to do?'

'I'd just like to have it nice,' Mum said, but would not look Dad in the eye.

Dad made no effort to get started but Mum bought cans of paint and began on the room herself. She shifted furniture and dragged the stepladders upstairs with grunts and groans of distress until she shamed Dad into taking over. 'And make a good job of it,' she said as she passed him the brushes.

'Have I ever done anything else?' Dad said indignantly.

When he had finished, late on Sunday night, he said to Mum, 'Are you going to tell us now?'

'Tell you what?' said Mum.

'Why all this fuss? Who's it for? Your precious Wallace?' he added jokingly.

'Yes, if you must know,' Mum replied.

'What!' Dad exclaimed. He closed his eyes in horror, stumbled against the stepladders and fell headlong downstairs. He picked himself up with a groan. 'It can't be true. Tell me I'm dreaming, Angie.'

'That's what Mum said, Dad. You've done it for Wallace Windle.'

'I'll undo it then,' he said with a roar and

collapsed in a heap, his hand to his back. 'Ow!' he yelled in agony. 'Now see what you've done.'

'Are you all right, dear?' Mum said.

'No. I'm not all right. I've wasted a weekend, I've broken my back, and my wife has gone off her head.' He tried to stand but was only able to support himself on all fours.

'Get up, dear. There's no need for all this fuss just because I've asked Wallace ... to spend Christmas with us.'

'Oh, Mum!' said Angie. 'Christmas is usually so nice.'

'And why shouldn't it be nice this year? Nicer than ever probably.' She examined the spare room. 'Yes, I think it will do.'

Dad crawled upstairs.

'Can I help you, Dad?' Angie said.

He ignored her, moved on hands and knees towards the spare room, a mean look on his face and grabbed a paint brush.

'No, you don't,' Mum said. 'Do what you like to it after Wallace has gone but I want it nice for him.' She stood, hands on hips, protecting the room.

'Are you in pain, Dad?' Angie asked.

He got to his feet without difficulty. 'Only from

a broken heart,' he said and clasped his hands to his chest in a very Windle-like gesture. 'Help me to my couch, dear lady.' He put his hand on his wife's arm in a gesture of helplessness. She thrust him away but Angie saw the suspicion of a smile in her eyes.

'Why?' Angie asked her mother later. 'Why invite him for Christmas?'

'Poor man,' Mum said. 'Such a sweet and forgiving man. The world has passed him by. His old friends have turned from him, and his wife doesn't understand him.'

'His wife?'

'His fourth wife, and the others were the same.'

'But why us?'

Mum looked at Angie in surprise. 'Because I do understand him. Christmas can be a lonely time for anyone as sensitive as Wallace.'

It won't be the same, thought Angie. 'When's he coming?'

'The day before Christmas Eve. He's resting, he says.'

'Resting?'

'Not working. It's hard for a man of such talent as Wallace. He can't be expected to take any sort of part. We must make him welcome.'

'What about Goliath?' said Angie. 'He can't stand the man.'

'Angie! Mr Windle to you! We'll put Goliath in a cattery over the holiday.'

'Send Goliath away! Over Christmas! Then I'll go too. I'd rather stay in a cattery with Goliath than here with Wallace Windle.'

When Dad heard Mum's idea of getting Goliath out of the way for the sake of Wallace Windle, he said firmly, 'That cat stays. If he goes, I go.'

Angie looked at him in surprise. 'We'll all go together,' he said, 'and leave Mum to keep Wallace company on her own.' He winked at Angie. 'That should give the neighbours something to talk about.'

'All right,' said Mum. 'But you'll have to keep him under control, Angie.'

'Who?' said Dad. 'Wallace Windle?'

Mum stormed off.

6 . . .

Angie enjoyed the preparations for Christmas, putting up decorations, making mince pies, choosing presents for Mum and Dad. It was fun.

But this year the thought of Wallace Windle took the edge off things. 'We'll just have to make the best of it,' she said to Goliath.

Goliath paid no attention. He had seen Dad bringing in a large turkey. His eyes followed every movement, watching to see where the bird was put. He licked his lips.

'Goliath,' Angie said, reading his mind. 'You'll get your share – when it's cooked.'

Mum darted about the house, making sure everything was fit for the coming of Wallace Windle. She came downstairs after her eighth inspection of the premises. 'The guest room looks very nice,' she said.

'Guest room?' enquired Dad. 'Oh, you mean the spare room. We *are* going up in the world.'

'There's no harm in trying to make the best of ourselves,' said Mum. 'I hope you've left the

lounge tidy.'

'Lounge, is it?' Dad said. 'I thought it was the living-room.'

Mum turned her back on him and went to the front door to await the arrival of her hero.

'I hope nothing happens to stop him coming,' Mum said when Angie joined her. 'He did say he might have a call from his agent about a big part in a play.' She sighed. 'I'm so looking forward to having him with us. It's a dream come true.'

Round the corner a small portly man, in a broad-brimmed hat, appeared, carrying two large suitcases. He stopped to rest, put the cases down and sat on one of them.

'It's him,' cried Mum. 'It's Wallace. Go and get your father to help the poor man.' She rushed towards Wallace Windle, took him by the hand, led him to the house and told Dad, when he appeared at the door, 'Fetch Wallace's things while I show him to his room.'

Dad, mouth agape, looked at Angie. 'Fetch Wallace's things! I'll be hanged if I do!'

'You'll be hanged if you don't,' said Angie. 'I'll help you.'

They went to pick up the suitcases. 'This one weighs a ton,' Dad said.

'So does this,' said Angie.

'He's come for a month,' Dad said.

'At least,' said Angie

'Oh no,' said Dad. 'I think I'll emigrate.'

They carried the cases up to the spare room.

'Thank you, darlings,' Windle said. 'Put them there.' He looked around the room. 'I wonder, my dear Rosemary, if I could impose on you to find me a slightly larger room? I'm so used to large dressing-rooms, as the star, you know? You do understand, my dear dear Rosemary.' He took hold of her hands between his and held them to his chest.

Mum looked at Dad.

'No,' he said. 'I'm not giving up our room.'

'Oh, my goodness, darling,' Windle said to him. 'Of course not. Displace the man of the house, my dear? It's unthinkable.'

Mum looked at Angie. Angie stared in front, determined not to give way either.

'Angie?' Mum said.

'What?'

'It won't take you long to clear your room, will it?' Mum's eyes pleaded. 'Angie?'

For Mum's sake, she would give up her room, but she hoped it would give that odious man nightmares, sleeping there. She angrily collected her things, carried them to the 'guest room', and piled them on the bed. Wallace had gone downstairs and she could hear his voice in the 'lounge', swelling and booming, filling the house with its theatrical rise and fall.

She wondered where Goliath was. He must be out not to have responded to Windle's arrival.

She went to find him. 'Goliath!' she yelled when she saw him in the kitchen. He had dragged the turkey from the larder and now stood growling over it, challenging her to take it from him.

She grabbed him, put him out of the back door, dusted the turkey down and returned it to the larder. The teeth marks wouldn't show once the bird was cooked.

Goliath howled outside. Angie decided he was in the right sort of mood to meet Wallace. She let him in, picked him up and took him to the lounge. She opened the door and pushed him in, closed it behind him, and waited.

The actor's declamation changed to a cry of terror, a frenzied 'Get him away! Get him away!'

'Get him off, Dad,' Mum said.

'Me?'

'Angie!' Mum called. 'Come and rescue him,'

Angie, smug with delight, opened the door to see Wallace Windle cowering behind the settee, hands over his head, protecting his toupee. Goliath crouched along the back of the settee snarling with ill-will.

'Do something, Angie,' Mum said. 'He won't let me near him.'

Angie took hold of Goliath by the scruff of the neck and spoke firmly to him. His growl changed

to a purr as she took him from the room.

'Keep him away from me,' Wallace shouted after her.

'And a merry Christmas to you too,' she said under her breath.

'I'll have to take you to see Tommy for an hour or so,' she explained. Goliath continued purring. Now that he'd shown that creature what he thought of him he was willing to behave himself – for the time being.

There was another old Wallace Windle film on television that afternoon. Mum insisted on watching it and Wallace was pleased to see himself. 'My dear Rosemary,' he said. 'What joy it is to see the pleasure I give. How rewarding to know how moved you are by my poor performance.'

Mum sighed and told him his performance was perfection itself.

'You are too kind, my dear, too kind.'

Angie and Dad slipped away.

'What's got into her, Angie? Taken in by such nonsense,' Dad said. 'His speeches are as artificial as his hair.'

Angie sniggered. 'It moves by itself.'

'Goliath thought it was alive. What are we to

do? I can't stand the man.'

'We have to put up with him for Mum's sake. Christmas will soon be over.'

'But will he go then?' said Dad. 'I have the most awful feeling about it.'

'We can always set Goliath on him,' Angie said and wondered if that might work.

'There's an idea,' said Dad. 'But you're right. For Mum's sake we have to put up with him, awful though he is.'

7 . . .

Goliath was refused entry into the lounge. Mum told Angie to keep him away until he had learnt some manners. Wallace Windle established himself in Goliath's easy chair while Dad, glowering, sat again in the high-backed chair.

Angie had been invited to a party and was glad to get away from their guest. He was bad enough on the screen; in the flesh – and there was a lot of it – he was dreadful.

When she got home Goliath met her at the door and led her upstairs. He stopped at Wallace Windle's bedroom door. From within snorts and snores came in alternate rushes followed by a moment's silence, like the unwilling start of a car engine. Goliath hurled himself at the door handle.

'No, Goliath,' Angie said. The sounds redoubled in volume. 'Grrr, guggle, guggle, grrr.' Silence. Then it began again. 'Come on, Goliath,' she said and took him downstairs.

Her parents were in the lounge, not speaking to each other.

'What is it?' Angie said.

There was no answer.

'Has something happened?'

'Nothing to concern you,' Mum said sharply.

'Old Wallace has blotted his copy-book,' said Dad.

'Nothing of the sort,' said Mum. 'It was you, plying him with drink when it was obvious he was tired to begin with.'

'He's drunk?' Angie said.

'As a lord,' Dad told her. 'Legless. I had to put him to bed.'

'And it was your fault,' Mum said.

'I didn't drink a bottle of whisky. He did.'

'Only when you insisted.'

'I did nothing of the kind. It gave me no pleasure to see our Christmas drinks disappearing down the throat of that—'

'Don't say it,' interrupted Mum. 'He's a fine man. He has faults like anyone else. If he wants to forget his sorrows he's welcome to our drinks. And he has sorrows. I should know. He opened his heart to me.'

Dad frowned. 'I hope you didn't open yours to him.'

Mum turned pink. 'Of course not. Don't be

silly. It's time for bed. We've a lot to do tomorrow.'

The next day was Christmas Eve. Goliath was excited at the rich smells coming from the kitchen. And there was no Wallace Windle to infuriate him.

'Let Mr Windle lie in,' Mum said, but, in the middle of the morning, when Angie and Mum stopped for a coffee, Mum said, 'Perhaps we should wake him. Take him a cup of coffee, Angie.'

Angie went upstairs and knocked on the bedroom door. A steady droning, like the tuning of bagpipes, came from inside. She opened the door and peeped in.

A full set of false teeth grinned at her from a glass beside the bed. Then her eyes met a hairy creature clinging to the bedpost. She suppressed a scream and summoned up courage enough to look closer and saw the thing was Wallace Windle's toupee.

A bright bald pate slowly emerged from under the bedclothes, two bleary eyes opened, closed again, opened, and Wallace Windle sat up, grabbed the toupee, thrust it all awry upon his

head, dipped his hand into the glass to get his false teeth, turned away from her and turned back, mouth full.

'Little secrets,' he said. 'Shall we keep them to ourselves?'

'A cup of coffee,' she said to explain her presence.

'Ah, how kind!' His voice was rough and rasping, his face blotchy, his cheeks sunken, his mouth slack and a stale smell of whisky lingered on his breath.

'It's after eleven o'clock,' Angie said, going to

the door.

'So early!' He slid back under the bedclothes.

'How is he this morning, Angie?' Mum said.

As horrible as yesterday, Angie wanted to say, but she answered, 'He seems very tired. I don't think we'll be seeing him for an hour or two.'

'Oh dear,' said Mum. 'I hope he's all right. Later I'll do him something light, to tempt his appetite.'

His appetite needed no tempting. He came downstairs just as they sat down to eat. Dad had left work early to join them for the midday meal.

'Ah,' said Wallace, seeing them at the table. 'What a joy a family is! How we men of the theatre miss the simple pleasures!' He pulled up a chair, reached for a plate, filled it with vegetables and handed it to Dad for a portion of the ham Dad was carving. Then hungrily he wolfed his meal and was ready for more.

'Don't forget Goliath,' Angie reminded Dad as he carved more slices for the actor.

Wallace Windle looked round in alarm.

'You're quite safe,' Angie said. 'We've locked him in the kitchen.'

'It's just a superstition of mine,' Wallace said.

'There's an old theatre saying "never share a scene with children or animals". The same goes for life off-stage too. I can't stand children or animals, I'm afraid.'

Angie looked at Mum. They had agreed to have Tommy for the afternoon while Mrs Roberts took the rest of her family shopping.

'Go and tell Mrs Roberts we can't have Tommy, Angie,' Mum said.

'That's not fair,' Angie said. 'Tommy's looking forward to it.'

'Do as I say,' Mum ordered.

'I'll see he gets in no one's way,' Angie said.

Mum reluctantly agreed to let Tommy come, but she took Angie aside and warned her, 'Don't let Tommy near Mr Windle. He is our guest remember.'

So is Tommy, Angie said, but not aloud.

Angie took Tommy and Goliath up to her bedroom and stayed with them. They were happy together, agreed on everything except Wallace Windle. Tommy loved his appearances on TV. Goliath loathed them.

Sound from the television reached them now and Angie recognised the music as the opening to 'Southern Heat', Mum's particular favourite among Wallace Windle films.

Goliath pricked up his ears and Tommy crawled to the door. 'Out,' he said. 'Out.'

It could do no harm to let him see the film.

'Come on, Tommy,' she said. 'Not you, Goliath. You can't be trusted.'

She hesitated outside the lounge but Tommy was not to be denied. She carried him in. Wallace was staring with undisguised admiration as his features filled the screen. Tommy, chortling with delight, wriggled from Angie's grasp. He made his way across the floor, not to the television screen but to the real Wallace Windle, grabbed the actor's trouser legs and tried to pull himself up.

'Ow!' yelled Wallace. 'Get off! Get off!' He kicked out to loosen Tommy's hold, but it was no use. Tommy's grip was firm, friendly but firm. There was no dislodging him. Wallace's eyes bulged with horror as the child, all smiles and dribbles of joy, pulled himself up to his lap.

'Get him off! Get him off!' Wallace cried, desperate with terror. 'No! NO!'

Angie took hold of Tommy and with Mum's help freed the actor. He looked at Tommy's beaming face with revulsion.

'He likes you,' Mum said hesitantly. 'That's

why.'

Wallace closed his eyes. 'Dear, dear lady. Do not misunderstand me, but a soul as troubled as mine is in no state to undergo shocks like this. I warned you.'

'I know, Wallace. Forgive me. Take him away, Angie. Put him somewhere safe.'

Angie carried Tommy out. He hadn't taken offence. When he saw Goliath again he gurgled joyfully and Goliath welcomed him with ecstasy.

So, thought Angie, the actor's dislike of children was genuine. She must bear it in mind.

The rest of the day passed quietly. Angie took Tommy back to his mother and asked them to look after Goliath for a while. She had too much to do wrapping presents to keep watch on him.

'I hope you've bought something for Mr Windle,' Mum said.

'How was I to know he'd be here for Christmas?' she said.

'It wouldn't be kind to leave him out.'

'I'll buy him some vanishing cream – to make him vanish.'

'You horrid girl. Get him a box of cigars. I'll give you the money. Make a gesture. It is Christmas, a time of goodwill after all.'

'It doesn't feel like Christmas with him around.'

Mum looked ready to burst into tears. 'I can't think why you and Dad have taken against him so. He's a fine man. He's fallen on hard times. He needs understanding, sympathy, a bit of love.'

Angie stared at her mother. She meant it.

'Promise me something, Mum.'

'What, dear?'

'Please don't go in for any more competitions.'

8 . . .

Angie wanted to exchange presents straight after breakfast as always, but Mum insisted on waiting for Wallace.

Mum and Dad and Angie worked on the Christmas dinner and the actor slept. His snores rumbled through the house, driving Goliath to distraction until the mouth-watering smells from the kitchen became too strong to ignore. He crouched under the kitchen table, ready to snatch any morsel of turkey to come his way.

At last Wallace came down. Mum had put his presents together. There were three parcels – Angie's box of cigars, one from Mum herself and one, believe it or not, from Dad. At least that was what the label said. Angie guessed Dad knew little about it.

'Oh, darlings,' Wallace said. 'How good you are. And my own gifts for you have not yet arrived, except for this poor offering.' He handed a small package to Mum. 'This is for you, Rosemary, with heartfelt wishes for your good

66

fortune.' He leaned over to Mum and planted a kiss on her lips. Mum blushed, lowered her eyes, then glanced at Dad before opening Wallace's gift.

It was a bottle of perfume. Angie recognised it. It was hers. She had left it in a drawer in her bedroom. She opened her mouth to protest but, when she saw the pleasure in her mother's eyes, she said nothing but hoped Wallace would choke on his cigars.

He unwrapped each parcel with extravagant cries of joy. When he opened Angie's he came towards her with outstretched arms to kiss her too, but the look in her eyes warned him to keep his distance.

Angie wondered if he would thank Dad with a kiss. Dad saw the danger and put the table between him and Wallace. Wallace took hold of Dad's hand and shook it demonstratively. 'You make a lonely man happy with such thoughtfulness.' He took a large handkerchief from his pocket and wiped a tear from his eye. 'Forgive me,' he said. 'I am so touched.'

'We all are,' said Mum.

'Indeed we are,' said Dad. 'Touched.' He tapped a finger to his head, hiding his gesture from Mum, but she looked at him with an angry frown and a warning to behave.

Wallace enjoyed his Christmas dinner, grunting with appreciation at each mouthful, extending his plate for second and third helpings, pushing his glass towards Dad for frequent refills of wine. At the end of the meal he sat back, belched, lit a cigar and watched as Angie and Dad cleared the table and retired to the kitchen.

'I'll never forgive your mother,' Dad said. 'Wishing that monster on us.'

Mum put her head round the door. 'Be quiet,' she said. 'He's asleep. We mustn't disturb him.'

'He's had a hard morning,' Dad commented pointedly as he cleaned a saucepan.

'You'd better go for your walk,' Mum said. 'Perhaps you'll be better-natured when you get back.'

'Aren't you coming, Mum?' said Angie. Every Christmas they went for a walk after dinner. It was a family tradition.

'I can't leave Wallace on his own.'

'Put Goliath in with him to keep him company,' said Dad. 'That should entertain him.'

Mum flounced out of the kitchen.

'Touched,' Dad said. 'We're all touched. And Mum's bewitched. I don't understand it. Till now, apart from her competitions, she's been a sensible woman. Now, I just don't know. Come on, Angie, let's go for our walk.'

Wallace Windle was still asleep when they got back. Mum put a finger to her lips to urge them to be quiet. Dad ignored her, switched on the radio and turned up the volume.

Mum moved quickly to switch it off, but it was too late. Wallace was opening his eyes. 'Tea-time already?' he said, patting his stomach. 'You spoil me, my dear.' He beamed contentedly. 'Just a

little Christmas cake, some sherry trifle maybe, turkey sandwiches, sausage rolls, mince pies. Not very much after that splendid lunch.'

Dad touched his forelock, bowed humbly and said, 'Certainly, Mr Windle, and a bottle of champagne to wash it down?' He was showing signs of rebellion.

'Why, yes,' said Wallace. 'What an excellent

idea! Champers is always welcome, darling.'

Dad looked abashed. Mum took his arm and led him outside.

'Where will you find champagne today?' she said.

'I didn't think he'd take me seriously!' Dad exclaimed.

'Well he did and you can't disappoint him,' said Mum.

'Can't I?' challenged Dad.

'No. You can't. Go and find some. I leave it to you. But find some you must.'

Dad knew when he was beaten. He put on his coat and set off.

He returned an hour later with a bottle of champagne. 'I've been thinking,' he said to Angie. 'I'll poison it, let him see he's not wanted.'

'But he is,' said Angie. 'Mum wants him.'

'I can't understand it. He's cast some sort of spell on her.'

'He won't be with us much longer. After all he's only come for Christmas. It's Boxing Day tomorrow and the day after that he'll be gone.'

Dad shook his head. 'I reckon he knows when he's on to a good thing. He'll not give that up so easily.'

They all felt sleepy especially Goliath. He had had more than his fair share of turkey, having found a way of opening the larder. He made no effort to get into the lounge, preferring to stay where the food was. Angie kept him company for much of the evening. She could not bear the sight of Wallace Windle stretched out, hands over his paunch, smug smile on his fat face.

'He looks as if he's there for good,' she complained to Goliath.

Goliath growled as if he shared her feelings.

'We'll have to do something, Goliath.'

She went to say good-night and opened the lounge door. The television was on but no one was watching it. Wallace Windle was sleeping, Dad was staring moodily at a book and Mum was darning a sock.

'What on earth are you doing, Mum?' Angie exclaimed.

'Ssh,' Mum whispered. 'What does it look like? I'm darning socks.'

'On Christmas Day?'

'The poor man's got none to wear.'

'Oh, they're his,' Angie said with disgust.

Wallace Windle's eyes opened a fraction and closed quickly again. He knows what I think of

him, she thought, and he's not worried.

'Good-night,' she said. 'Good-night, Mum, Dad. Good-night, Wallace.'

Wallace pretended to wake. 'Oh, good-night, dear heart. How I envy the young their untroubled sleep. Sleep well, my dear.'

Untroubled sleep! She was too furious to sleep, trying to think of ways to make Wallace's short stay uncomfortable. Short stay? She hoped Dad's fears that Wallace would linger on after Christmas were ill-founded.

She heard scratching at the door and opened it to see Goliath. He stalked in and settled down on her bed. She let him stay. He had suffered enough in his banishment from the lounge.

'What are we going to do, Goliath?'

Goliath curled up beneath the eiderdown and purred as if he knew the answer.

9 . . .

Boxing Day passed without the usual family out-
ings. 'We can't leave Wallace on his own,' Mum
said, 'not when he's leaving tomorrow.'

'Are you sure?' Dad said.

Mum looked anxious. 'That was the arrange-
ment. You don't think—?' She seemed to be
having second thoughts about Wallace Windle.
'He's expecting news about an important part.
He'll go home for that.'

But Wallace showed no signs of going. Instead
he brought down a bundle of dirty clothes and
said to Mum, 'I felt sure you wouldn't mind
putting these in with the family wash, Rosemary.'

Mum had had no intention of doing a family
wash that day.

'You're so kind, my dear. One or two delicate
things will need careful treatment. And I do like
my shirts to be well-laundered.' He pressed
Mum's hand to his lips. 'I'm expecting an aud-
ition for a rather important part. I must look my
best.'

'Have you heard?' Mum asked.

'Not yet, dear lady. But I left this address with my agent. I expect to hear shortly.'

'Shortly?' said Dad.

'When's shortly?' Angie said.

'Who can tell?' Wallace said. 'Today? Tomorrow? The day after? Who knows?'

'This year, next year, sometime, never,' Dad said to Angie when they went into the yard to get away from him.

'We must do something,' Angie said.

'The cheek of the man, taking advantage of Mum like that!' Dad said. 'What can we do?'

'Tell him to go. You're the one to do that.'

'Your mother would never forgive me.'

'She's fed up with him too.'

'But she won't admit it. And she's too soft-hearted.'

Goliath joined them and wound around Angie's legs until she picked him up. He had a self-satisfied smile on his face.

'You've been at the turkey,' Angie accused him.

'What was left after that man had finished,' Dad said. 'Have you ever seen an appetite like his?'

'Only Goliath's,' said Angie.

'Goliath,' said Dad.

'And Tommy,' said Angie.

They smiled at each other.

'Children and animals, he said, didn't he? Couldn't stand them,' said Dad.

'Tommy and Goliath.'

'Goliath and Tommy.'

They went into the house. Wallace was in the living-room, sitting in the easy chair. He was smoking a cigar and had a glass of whisky by his side, the last of the Christmas drinks.

'Comfortable?' Dad asked.

'Eminently, darling. Who could wish for more?'

'That's nice,' said Dad, nodding to Angie. She knew what to do. Mum was in the kitchen, wrinkling up her nose at the state of Wallace's clothes. She looked ruefully at Angie. 'I didn't think,' she began.

'It won't be long now,' Angie said.

'What are you up to?' Mum said distrustfully.

'Nothing, Mum. I'm just going to borrow Tommy. Goliath needs someone to play with.'

Mum shook her head in disbelief.

Tommy's mother was glad to be relieved of him for a while. 'He's a handful,' she said. 'Always on the go.'

'Don't disturb Wallace,' Mum said on Angie's return. 'You know what he feels about children.'

Angie took Goliath and Tommy to her room and left them to entertain each other while she went to see how Wallace and Dad were doing.

The actor beckoned her in with a fulsome gesture. 'Come in, dear young lady,' he said. 'I was telling your father of my last triumph. Romeo! What a part! And what a performance! Such a reception!'

'Romeo?' she said incredulously.

Wallace looked crossly at her. 'I've played all the great roles in my time – Hamlet, Richard the Third, yes and Romeo.'

Dad guffawed and covered up by coughing. 'A glass of water, please,' he managed to say.

Angie went for a glass of water. 'Romeo!' Dad whispered and broke into a fit of the giggles again. Wallace glared. He sat in his chair like a stranded whale, bloated, pale and gasping.

'Now's the time,' Dad said softly.

She went upstairs, took Tommy in her arms and, calling Goliath to follow her, went down to the living-room. She opened the door. Wallace Windle lay back in his chair, talking of his successes on the boards. 'To be or not to be,' he declaimed.

He turned and saw Tommy, and then Goliath. The child chuckled with delight, the cat bared its teeth. Wallace blenched, gulped, held his hands in front of him in horror to fend off the threat.

'No,' he said. 'Please, no. Take them away.'

Angie put Tommy down and he scrambled across the floor to the actor, pulled himself up to Wallace's lap and planted a wet kiss on his cheek. Wallace gave a strangled cry of loathing and tried to push the child away.

Goliath bided his time. Angie watched him, ready to pluck him away if he became dangerous. She didn't want him to hurt Wallace, only frighten him off.

Wallace had forgotten the cat in his struggle to free himself from the adoring Tommy. He looked at Angie in appeal, then at Dad. 'Please,' he said in such anguished tones that Angie was tempted to rescue him, but a warning glance from Dad held her back.

Tommy was not to be denied. He reached up his podgy arms to clasp Wallace about the neck. Wallace tried to hold him away, but there was no resisting the child, He stroked Wallace's cheeks, then his fat fingers moved to Wallace's hair to fondle that. It came away in his hand. Tommy opened his mouth in surprise and threw the wig away in revulsion.

It did not reach the ground. Goliath leapt, caught it in his claws and began to fight it, tearing with his formidable fangs at the hairy thing.

'Oh, my God!' said Wallace. He stood up and Tommy slid to the ground. 'Get it from him.' He

bent down to grab his toupee but Goliath was in no mood to let it go. He growled and clawed and bit and tore at the wig until it was spread in tufts about the room. Only when nothing remained but the lining did Goliath let his catch go. Tommy, with a cherubic smile, held it up to Wallace.

The door opened and in came Mum. 'What's going on?' she exclaimed when she saw the scraps of hair, here, there and everywhere. Then she saw Wallace. For a second Angie thought Mum was

going to burst out laughing, but she controlled herself and took command.

'Put Goliath out, Angie, take Tommy to his mother and bring a brush and tidy up. Give Wallace a drink, Dad. You can tell he's had a nasty shock. And when you've recovered, Wallace, you must give me some advice about your shirts. I shall have to put buttons on, do some minor repairs. I need to know which you want first.'

For once the actor's theatrical manner deserted him. 'I don't know why you are so good to me, I really don't.'

Wallace spent the rest of the day in his bedroom, not even coming down for meals.

'He won't open the door to me,' Mum said. 'You'll have to take him something, Dad. He might not mind facing you.'

Dad returned to say Wallace wanted only quiet to prepare himself for the part he expected.

'What can it be, I wonder?' Mum said.

'Romeo?' Dad said and burst out laughing. Mum glared him into silence.

'I don't know how you could be so cruel,' Mum said to Angie. 'And you shouldn't have let her,' she said to Dad.

'We were thinking of you,' he said.

'I can look after myself,' Mum replied. 'And as for you, Goliath, I'm ashamed of you.' Goliath settled in the easy chair, closed his eyes and purred.

10 . . .

'There's a letter for Mr Windle,' Angie said.

'Take it up to him, dear. It'll be the one he's expecting, from his agent.'

'Your letter, Mr Windle,' Angie called and knocked on the door.

The door opened a fraction and a hand came out to take the letter. The door closed. Angie called, 'Your shirts are ready, mended and ironed.'

The door opened again, wide enough for Wallace's face to appear. He was wearing a nightcap.

'Good news?' she said.

'Indeed it is, my dear.' He sounded more his old self. 'A part in a thousand. My only regret is that I must cut my visit short. I had hoped to spend so much more time with you all.' He peeped out of the room, looking this way and that. 'You've got that monster under control, I hope.'

'Goliath? Oh yes.'

'And that dreadful child?'

'Tommy will be sorry to see you go. You're his hero.'

'The penalty of fame,' Wallace said. 'Tell your mother I'll be leaving in an hour or so. I'll slip away without saying good-bye. It would be too heart-breaking. Tell her I shall treasure the memory of her sweet nature for ever. Say,' he paused for effect. 'Say I shall always have her in mind as my Juliet when I play Romeo.'

'Romeo? Is that the part?' Angie said with

astonishment.

'Who knows what fate has in store?'

Angie told her mother Wallace was getting ready to leave. Dad had gone to work.

'He says he'll slip away without saying good-bye.'

'He'll do no such thing.' Mum was indignant. 'After all, we may never see him again. I want to thank him for bringing a little glamour into our lives.'

'Oh, Mum!'

'You must admit it was a different sort of Christmas.'

They heard a bumping on the stairs and saw Wallace dragging his suitcases down. His big black broad-brimmed hat shadowed his face and hid his baldness.

Angie took a suitcase, left the house and turned to wait for Wallace. He stood at the door, bending over Mum's hand, kissing it in an old-world gesture. For a moment he seemed about to sweep off his hat but he merely touched the brim, picked up the other suitcase and joined Angie.

'Where to?' she said.

'Just round the corner. I'll get a taxi.'

She stopped round the corner and put the

suitcase down. Wallace was already out of breath. 'Thank you, young lady. Have you ever thought of going on the stage?'

'No.'

'Don't, my dear.' He waved her away and blew her a kiss. She left him standing there. She supposed he had money for a taxi. When she heard a vehicle pull to a halt she went back to see Wallace struggling on to a bus with his cases. A fellow-passenger helped him.

Poor Wallace, she thought. I hope he gets the part. She would never know. Wallace had passed out of their lives.

Home was home once more. Goliath returned to the living-room; when Mrs Roberts wanted them to look after Tommy they were glad to do so. Mum no longer put on airs and Dad was his old self.

'No more competitions,' he demanded of Mum.

'No more,' she said. 'At least—'

'What is it?' Dad said in alarm.

'There is one I've entered, but it won't come to anything. And it's only for some theatre tickets.'

Angie had returned to her own room after giving it a good airing to get rid of the smell of cigars. Everything was more or less as she had left it, apart from the missing perfume and Mum had that.

She couldn't find the four-leaved clover. But since Mum had given up competitions – if she really had – they could do without the luck it brought.

And it had not been all good luck. It had brought Wallace Windle.

When Angie went shopping with Mum, just before reaching the till Mum grabbed a tin of curry powder. 'Win a trip to the Taj Mahal,' Angie read on the label.

'Dad doesn't like curry,' Angie said.

Mum looked guilty. 'He should try something different every now and again,' she said.

'You promised.'

'Just one more,' Mum pleaded.

Angie replaced the curry powder on the shelf. 'It would be a waste of time anyway. Wallace Windle has taken the four-leaved clover.'

'I gave it to him, Angie. His need is greater than ours. He hasn't worked for years. When I chose him as the actor I most wanted to have dinner with, it came as a life-saver, he told me. Everyone in the business thought he was dead. I brought him luck.

I hope it lasts and he gets the part.'

'Perhaps he'll write and tell us,' Angie said. But no word came from him and soon Wallace was no more than a memory.

'I've won!' Mum announced proudly one morning in late January.

'Oh no!' Dad said. 'Who is it this time?'

'Not who. What. A box at the Theatre Royal with a champagne supper.'

'What's on?' said Angie.

Dad looked at the tickets. 'A pantomime,' he said. 'I love pantomimes and it's Jack and the Beanstalk, one of my favourites.'

They dressed in their best finery. Dad insisted on their taking a taxi to the theatre door, and there the manager met them and showed them to their box. Opera glasses were provided and a bottle of champagne was opened.

'This is grand,' said Dad.

'You see,' said Mum, inclining her head to the audience from time to time, like royalty. 'Competitions can work out well.'

The lights dimmed, the orchestra began to play and the curtains parted to show a thatched cottage, Jack the 'principal boy', and a cow. Angie remembered the story of Jack going to the market to sell a cow and meeting someone who persuaded him to exchange it for a bag of beans.

Daisy, the cow, was a most wilful creature. Its back legs did not work in harmony with its front legs, so that, as the hind legs moved backwards and the front legs forward, the cow collapsed on all fours.

'It's going to come apart,' Dad whispered.

But it didn't come apart. It skittered around the stage to the delight of the children and the frustration of the man who bought it from Jack. It refused to do anything expected of it, clattered to the front of the stage, bowed to the orchestra, did a little dance and left the stage to thunderous applause, returning immediately to take a bow, first kneeling with its front legs, then its back.

Dad was red-faced with laughter. 'Sheer genius!' he said. 'I've not laughed so much in years.'

Whenever the cow returned to the stage it was greeted with loud cheers. When it left, a great sigh arose, at which it reappeared, took a bow, kicked up its legs and departed.

After the interval the cow was not seen so often but, just before the finale, it pranced on to the stage, fell over itself, rolled over to have its tummy tickled (just as Goliath did) and capered madly from side to side of the stage till it was finally re-united with Jack's mother.

'It's the star of the show,' Dad said. 'I see why Wallace Windle doesn't like appearing with animals. That cow can act.'

'It's not an animal,' said Mum.

'Of course it's not an animal,' Dad said. 'But it's sheer genius just the same.'

The company gathered for the final colourful chorus. Angie looked through her glasses to see the actors in close-up. The principal boy was very pretty, the Giant very fierce, and the cow was just a cow.

Then each of the principal actors came forward to take their applause.

'Daisy!' the children shouted, insisting on the cow coming forward too. 'Daisy!'

Daisy ambled to the footlights, its legs still in disharmony and the crowd laughed and cheered. Then the cow divided, back legs from front, to reveal the actors who had amused them so. The front legs took off the cow's head and showed the glistening features of a fair-haired jovial young man.

From the cow's hind legs also emerged a face, the performer took a bow, raised a hand to wave to the audience, bowed again to renewed cheers, linked hands with the front legs, and did a scampering dance before taking his place with the rest of the cast.

'I don't believe it,' said Dad.

But it was true.

'It's him,' said Angie. 'It's Wallace.'

Mum said nothing. She stared through her glasses at the stage. The company took another bow and the curtain came down for the last time.

They travelled home, each filled with their own thoughts.

'He got his part, then,' Dad said.

'Not Romeo,' said Angie.

'The back end of a cow,' said Dad. 'But he was good. Better than he would have been as Romeo.'

Mum said nothing. 'I'll make coffee,' she said, keeping her feelings under control. Angie followed her into the kitchen.

'It was a lovely evening, Mum,' she said. 'I'm glad you won that competition.'

Mum smiled. 'He was good, wasn't he? Even as part of a cow.'

'The back end,' said Angie.

They went into the living-room with the coffee and paused, astonished, on the threshold.

Dad was in his old chair and on his lap, purring with contentment, was Goliath.

'I told him,' said Dad.

'What?' Angie said.

'I told him Wallace Windle had got his part, as the back end of a cow. He seemed to think it funny. He let me have my chair back.' He stroked the cat. 'I suppose we've got your competitions to thank for one thing. It brought us Goliath.'

'I've been thinking,' Mum said. 'We'll try curry

for dinner tomorrow.'

Here we go again, thought Angie.